SUE PURKISS
Changing Brooms

Jess longs to train to become a proper
witch, but her family can't afford the
tuition fees, and so she's stuck being
apprenticed to Agnes Moonthistle, whose
services as a witch aren't at all in demand –
because she's not very good. When the
TV programme, *Changing Brooms*, offers the
chance to use magic to win
ten thousand pounds, Jess may have
found her escape route at last …

First published 2004 by
A & C Black Publishers Ltd
37 Soho Square, London, W1D 3QZ

www.acblack.com

ISBN 0-7136-6858-X

A CIP catalogue for this book is available from the British Library.

A&C Black uses paper produced with elemental chlorine-free
pulp, harvested from managed sustained forests.

Printed and bound in Spain by G. Z. Printek, Bilbao.

SUE PURKISS
Changing Brooms

Illustrated by Lynne Chapman

A & C Black • London

For Anne Parsons and Christine Allen –
with many, many thanks

Mill Farm,
Crumpet Thrubwell

28 April

Dear Daughter,

I am just writing these few lines to wish you a
happy Beltane, which Hag Harriet tells me is a
very important day for you witches, being the
beginning of summer and all. I went to see
Harriet this morning, to ask her advice about
your brother Joe, who is still up to his old
tricks at school.

She asked me to send you her very best,
and to say to you that behind every cloud
there's another one. Or sometimes not.
Whatever she meant by that I don't know, but
perhaps you do.

Anyway, please remember me to cousin
Agnes. I hope you are behaving yourself and not

giving any cause for displeasure. We are all very proud of you, you know that. It will be a fine thing to have a witch in the family, and we are very grateful to Agnes for giving you such an opportunity.

Emmy and Archie are doing well at school, and Lucy keeps me busy but I don't mind because she's such a little sweetie, unlike her big brother, but the less said about him the better. Dad sends his best and says to tell you that the hens are laying better than ever, and he thinks it's because of something you said to them.

Much love,
Mother

Jess put the letter down on the kitchen table, smiling fondly. For a moment, she felt just as if she were at home, with the twins and Lucy running in and out and her mother shouting at Joe because he'd not done his jobs and telling her father off for forgetting to wipe his feet. But her smile soon faded. She wasn't at home. She was miles away, in Melton Magna, where she was apprenticed to a distant relation of her mother's called Agnes Moonthistle.

Agnes was a weatherwitch, and she'd nobly offered to help the Frasers out by taking Jess off their hands – for a small but regular monthly consideration which they could barely afford – and teach her the profession. Jess would far rather have waited till she could have trained with Hag Harriet, who was a highly-skilled megawitch and very much in demand. Jess knew she could be a really good witch. She could feel the power within her, and she knew that Harriet would be the ideal person to teach her how to use it. But Harriet had no spaces for years to come, so Agnes's offer had been gratefully received.

Unlike Harriet, Agnes wasn't greatly in demand, because she really wasn't very good. If you asked her for a bit of gentle rain you might get anything from a thick sea mist to a hailstorm, which made farmers think carefully about hiring her a second time.

The first hint Jess had that business wasn't exactly booming was when she arrived at Agnes's house for the first time a year ago. It was dingy and dirty and had scary things lurking in corners. Jess later discovered that these were the left over evidence of a spell Agnes had tried, which was supposed to turn rats into domestic servants. It had, of course, gone horribly wrong – even a megawitch wouldn't be able to manage that, and Agnes was a long way off being a megawitch. It was after the rat incident that she'd decided to take on an apprentice to do the dirty work.

But Jess didn't just have to do the dirty work. She easily picked up the basics of weatherwitchery from Agnes, and soon became much better at it than Agnes herself, so that before long people began to ask specially for her instead. Today, for instance, she'd spent most of the afternoon at Reg Sowerby's, working on a weather charm for his strawberries. It was difficult, because he wanted sun for them but rain for his vegetables – but not too much, else it would swamp them. She'd felt like suggesting he should go and buy a hosepipe for his vegetables and a sun-lamp for his strawberries, but that wouldn't have been good for business so she'd bitten her tongue and got on with the job. It had been hard work, and she was looking forward to a rest.

Just as she'd finished reading her letter, Agnes came into the kitchen.

'Now Jess, you could have got back a bit earlier. I want you to bake a cake.'

'Oh, are we having a feast for Beltane?' asked Jess hopefully.

'No, we're going to watch *Changing Brooms* round at Sybil's, like we always do on a Thursday.'

This felt very unfair. Why couldn't Agnes have made a cake herself? After all, she was the one who'd been at home all day.

'All right,' she said, 'but it'll have to be a magic one. There's no time for anything else.'

'Oh, don't be such a show-off,' snapped Agnes, who was jealous because this was one of the many spells she'd never managed to master. 'Anyway, there's nothing clever about making a cake that only looks good. You know perfectly well that magic food doesn't taste of anything. Just make one quickly. I'll go on, and you can come round when it's done. Don't be too long.'

Wearily, Jess started to get the baking things out. Her letter was still on the table, and she picked it up, smoothing it with her fingers.

'I want to be a good witch, like Harriet,' she whispered. 'And I can be, I know it. But it's not going to happen if I stay here with Agnes. There has to be another way!'

A sudden breeze swirled through the window, bringing with it a scent of summer. Jess smiled, and murmured a few words. A hazy cloud scudded away from the sun, looking slightly surprised, and the sun responded with a burst of glorious evening light. Jess looked hard at the cake tin and pointed a finger at it. Instantly, it filled up with a warm, fragrant carrot cake.

'Great,' she said. She loosened it with a knife and turned it out. A corner broke off and she picked it up and popped it into her mouth. She smiled happily.

'Yum,' she said. 'Oohh, I'm good. I'm just so good!'

She put it into a plastic box and went round to Sybil's.

Chapter Two

Sybil worked in futures. She had really drifted into witchcraft because it was something of a family tradition – her mother, aunt and grandmother had all been witches. Unfortunately she had soon discovered that although she worked hard at all her lessons and became reasonably proficient, she didn't excel in any particular area: she just didn't have much talent.

However, she managed to get by with writing regular columns for magazines and newspapers, making vague predictions which were bound to come true occasionally. Most of her advice was actually quite good, because it was based on a kind heart and a lot of experience. So in a small way, she was quite successful.

Where Agnes was tall and thin, Sybil was small and round. But Sybil had a certain style. She wore her hair in a neat bob; it was generally an interesting marmalade colour, though it sometimes veered towards red and was at the moment subtly streaked with pink. She often seemed a little flustered – as she did now – as if she wasn't quite sure where she should be, or what she should be doing.

Her house was not at all like Agnes's. It was neat and clean and pretty, with comfortable armchairs, co-ordinating wallpaper borders, curtains with pelmets and sashes, and a tasteful arrangement of dried flowers in a shiny black cauldron standing in the fireplace. There was a collection of antique glass balls arranged on a table, and a sleek black cat called Mulrooney. He had recently appeared from nowhere, as cats sometimes do, and proceeded to settle into the most comfortable chair, gracefully accepting offerings of poached salmon and cream from time to time from a rather puzzled Sybil. The other noticeable thing about Mulrooney was that when he chose, he could speak.

'Come in, Jess dear,' said Sybil as she opened the door. 'I've just seen the news, and it said about Beltane and all the parties there are. I'm so sorry, it must be very dull for you here, just watching television.'

Agnes looked affronted. 'Dull? What do you mean, dull? Television's not dull, it's exciting and glamorous! Don't be such a snob. And we've got a cake. Who needs parties? Take it into the kitchen, and then Sybil can put it on a plate.' She turned and went into the living room and they heard an angry yowl as Agnes battled it out with Mulrooney for the best chair, and won. 'Hurry up,' she called, 'it's nearly time for *Changing Brooms*.'

Changing Brooms was a hugely popular programme – it was certainly Agnes and Sybil's favourite. Each week, two witches swapped houses and had two days and a fixed budget to redecorate one of the rooms. They worked with a professional designer; the most popular was Lancelot Marchpane, who was much admired by many viewers on account of his long flowing shirt cuffs, piratical black curls and close-fitting leather trousers.

They were also allowed to use a fixed amount of magic – up to three charms or spells for each room. Sometimes, in the rush to finish on time, the results could be very funny: viewers loved it when the magic went wrong or the returning witch hated what the other had done to her room. Very occasionally, someone would be so angry that they would lash out with an unauthorised spell, and the viewing figures would rise dramatically for the next programme.

Agnes and Sybil were soon nibbling crisps and munching cake (there seemed to be no problem in the taste department, Jess noted with a secret smile) and cackling happily at the antics of this week's witches and designers.

Jess was glancing idly through one of Sybil's glossy magazines when she noticed a full page advert for the Collegium Witchorum. She sighed. Now if only she could go *there*! But that was so impossible that it had never even been considered. It was a specialist college for gifted and talented witches; a sizeable proportion went on to become megawitches, proficient not just in one, but in all the main areas of witchcraft. You had to be very good to get in. She was good, she knew that – but even if by some miracle she proved to be good enough, her family could never afford the fees.

She flicked through the rest of the magazine, put it down, and glanced at the television. The programme was nearly finished, and the presenter, Tiffany Taylor, was beaming happily at the camera.

'And now,' said Tiffany, 'we've got something new to tell you about. Loads of you apply to be on the programme, and of course, we can only choose a few. So for one special programme, we're going to open it out so that lots more of you can have a chance to do your stuff.

'The way it'll work is this. The competition's going to be called "Room for a Broom". Good, isn't it?' She beamed. 'Choose a room in your own home. Then design a makeover for it, just like on the programme – the difference is that you do the design, not a professional. Oh no,' she said, twinkling merrily, 'we know you'd all like to have Lance to help – but you *can't have him*!

'Send in your plan to us at *Changing Brooms* – and you don't have much time for this, we need them within a week. Then we'll choose the most interesting fifteen, you'll do the makeover, and we'll film it. They'll be shown on a specially extended programme, the last in the series, on Midsummer's Eve. And we'll have a telephone vote so that you, the viewers, can choose the winner.

'So, there we go. Exciting, eh? Remember, you have to be a witch to enter – it's that element of magic that the rest of us love. For a full set of rules, see next week's edition of *Inside the Box*. Oh—' Her huge blue eyes opened wide. '—I nearly forgot! There's a whopping great prize! The winning witch gets ten thousand pounds – just think what you could do with that!

'Well, that's all from us at *Changing Brooms* for now – see you next week! Same time, same channel – but a different place! Bye for now!'

And Tiffany faded away, to be replaced by shots of that week's transformed rooms. One was scarlet and purple, with flowing draperies that might possibly have hidden a bed, the other was pale blue and interesting, with driftwood, rope, and what seemed to be a small beach hut in the corner.

But Jess didn't notice the draperies or the beach hut. Ten thousand pounds! She didn't need to think about what she would do with it – she knew. She would be off, in two shakes of a cat's tail, to the Collegium Witchorum. No more housework, no more being bossed about: instead, the chance to learn lots of wonderful new spells, to make new friends – maybe she'd even become a megawitch. She'd be rich, famous, successful and happy – and all she had to do was decorate a room! She was fizzing with excitement – she'd go down to the village shop first thing to get a copy of the TV listings magazine with the rules. It had turned out to be a good Beltane after all. She'd found a way out!

Chapter Three

The next morning, Agnes appeared briefly for tea and toast. She didn't seem to have slept very well. Her hair looked like a very untidy bird's nest, and her eyes had a strange and wild stare.

'I'm extremely busy,' she said mysteriously, 'so I mustn't be interrupted. I want you to go down to the shop and fetch me a ruler and some pencils. Oh, and you might as well get a copy of *Inside the Box* while you're there,' she added.

'What about your appointments?' asked Jess. 'You were supposed to be going over to Roundhayes Farm later this morning to sort out that problem with the marshy field. And—'

'Yes, yes. Cancel it. Cancel everything. I'll sort it out later.'

Jess was doubtful. 'Mr Healey was very cross when he rang. He said it was your fault the field was marshy, because you made it rain for three days when he'd just asked for a couple of light showers. He said if—'

'Oh, never mind all that. If he makes too much fuss he'll have more than a downpour to worry about. Tell him I'm ill, or I've been called away. Or *you* go. I'm surprised he didn't ask for you anyway.' And with that, she disappeared back upstairs.

* * *

Jess's friend Grin was in the shop, buying pasties and chocolate for lunch. Grin was a couple of years older than Jess. Like her, he was an apprentice, but he was learning to be a woodworker, and he was training with his father.

They were the only two apprentices in the village; all the other children went to school. Jess sometimes felt a bit lonely when she saw them going off in giggling little groups, but she didn't know about all the things they talked about, like teachers and homework, and who was friends with whom. So she didn't have any way of joining in with them.

But Grin was nice and his parents were kind to Jess as well. Sometimes she went round there for tea, and it was almost as good as being at home – though not quite, of course. She was just telling him about the *Changing Brooms* competition when Sybil came in. She went straight over to the magazine shelf, not noticing Grin and Jess, who were on the other side of the shop. Then she went over to the shopkeeper, Mrs Raven.

'Do you have a large sketch pad, Mrs Raven? And a glue stick?'

Mrs Raven smiled a sugary smile. 'Of course, Madam Parsons.' Witches were often called 'madam' – it was sensible to show respect.

Mrs Raven found the things Sybil had asked for, and refused to take any payment for them. She owed Sybil a big favour – when a new supermarket had opened a few miles away, she and Agnes had concocted a maze charm, which fixed it so that people from Melton Magna who set off for the big shop found themselves unaccountably lost; whichever way they turned, every road led back to the village, and particularly to the shop. It had worked wonders for sales, and Sybil had said she wouldn't dream of accepting payment – much to Agnes's disgust – saying that it was for the good of the community.

'Morning, Sybil,' said Jess, as Sybil was on her way out.

Sybil jumped. 'Oh! I didn't see you there! I just came in to get some – er – drawing things. Dear me, is that the time? I must be getting on – bye, dear.'

As the door closed behind her, Jess's eyes narrowed. 'She's entering it. She must be. And I bet that's what Agnes was doing last night too. Now, why? What do they need the money for?'

'Everybody could use ten thousand pounds,' Grin pointed out. 'Come to that, why do you want it in particular?'

Jess told him. 'It'd be brilliant,' she said enthusiastically. 'Think what fun it'd be, to be at the Collegium!'

Grin was quiet. 'So you'd be going away?' he said.

'Well, yes. Obviously. But I've got to win the competition first. I'm going to go back and copy down the rules now, before I pass all this on to Agnes. You could help me! You're much better at arty stuff than I am.'

He didn't look very enthusiastic, but Jess was so taken up with herself that she didn't notice. She rushed home, letting herself in quietly so that Agnes wouldn't hear her and she'd have time to copy down the rules from the listings magazine. There were quite a few of them.

Changing Brooms
Room For a Broom
Competition Rules

1. You may use any room, but you must have the written permission of the owner if it is not your own.

2. Your design must have a theme.

3. Magic may only be used a maximum of three times during the course of the makeover.

4. You may have one assistant.

5. *Changing Brooms* will provide £200 for each of the fifteen finalists. No more than this may be spent. Anything currently in the house may be used or recycled.

6. The makeover must take place within two days, and will be supervised by an adjudicator sent by the programme.

7. Professional designers my not enter. Nor may employees of *Changing Brooms*.

8. Cheating will lead to disqualification. The decision of the adjudicators on this will be immediate and final.

9. Entries must be in by 8 May.

As soon as she'd finished, Jess took the magazine, ruler and pencils up to Agnes. She knocked on the door and waited, as she'd been told to.

'Who?' called Agnes, sounding harassed.

'It's just me, with the stuff you asked me to get.'

'Ah. Just a moment.' There was a rustling of paper, and then Agnes called, 'Enter!'

But the door wouldn't open.

'It's stuck or something,' Jess called.

'Oh, yes. Yes, I put a charm on it. Now let me see – how do I take it off again?' There was some muffled muttering, then, 'Door, open!' Nothing happened. 'Open, door!' Still nothing. More muttering. 'Oh, all right, you cantankerous bit of wood – please!'

The door burst triumphantly open, to reveal Agnes's room in all its dubious splendour. The décor was a subtle shade of dust with more than a hint of cobweb. Jess sneezed. Agnes took the things from her and put them on the dressing table, which usually held bottles of ancient perfume and make up, but now was buried under scraps of paper and what looked like cuttings from magazines. Jess moved nearer to get a closer look, but Agnes blocked her view.

'No! It's private.'

She'd moved fast, but not fast enough. The

cuttings were all pictures of rooms. She'd been right. Agnes, who up till now had been about as house proud as Attila the Hun, had taken to interior design.

The next question was whether Sybil was also entering. She would be far more of a threat, Jess knew. Her house had style. It might not be Jess's kind of style, but it was still style. She had absolutely no doubt about her ability at magic, but she had lots about her ability to design and decorate. If she was going to beat Sybil, let alone everyone else who entered, she was going to need help, and she knew just who to ask. Grin was practical and good at making things, and he was her best friend – in fact, at the moment, he was her only friend. He would help. She rushed round to see him.

Chapter Four

Grin was in the workshop behind the family house, standing at his workbench. He had a piece of wood in the vice, and was gently chipping away at it with a chisel and mallet. He was so absorbed in his task that he didn't notice Jess.

'What are you making?' she said after she'd been standing there for a while. Her voice came out louder than she meant it to, and he jumped.

'Jess, don't do that!' he said crossly. 'The chisel could have slipped and ruined the wood.'

'So?' she said. 'If it had, I could have fixed it.'

'What, with a spell?' he said scornfully.

She was stung. 'Yes, with a spell! In fact, I could probably finish the whole thing off for you in ten seconds if I wanted to!'

'Go on then – show me! Show me how a spell can carve a bird!'

She closed her eyes and concentrated hard. She'd never been taught how to do such a difficult thing as this, but she felt sure she could. What she had to do was probe the piece of wood with her mind. It was yew, she discovered, from a tree that had been growing for centuries in a churchyard. She focused on the structure of the wood. Part of it was a golden colour, and that was quite soft and easy to work, but the other part, which was much darker, was hard and would be difficult. But when it was done it would be smooth and glossy, with a clear, intricate grain. She could see how to do it – a little push here, a little push there – but suddenly, she realised that she couldn't do it.

Her eyes flew open, and she looked distressed.

'I can't,' she said in a small voice. 'I don't know what it has to look like. I don't know the shape of the bird's head, or how its wings join on to its body. And I don't know what its position should be, or how to make it fit this particular piece of wood. When I did it before, I made a pot out of a lump of clay. But I can't do this.'

'You've got your magic,' said Grin calmly, 'and I've got my craft. That's all it is. You have to know the wood. You have to know how to work it so it won't split, how to use the grain.'

'But it's not just that, is it?' she said slowly. 'It's having an idea of the shape you want to make. That's the bit I couldn't do.'

'Well, maybe I have some magic too. Just different magic,' he said, picking up the chisel again and angling it carefully. 'Anyway, I don't mean to be rude, but was there some particular reason why you dropped in? Only I've got a lot to do.'

Jess felt hurt. Why was he being so horrible? She realised more than ever that she needed his help, but how could she ask him when he was being like this? 'It's quite all right,' she said stiffly. 'You needn't worry. It wasn't anything in particular.'

She marched out of the workshop, her head held high. Grin watched. She nearly always wore her witch's hat; she'd told him once it was a sort of badge of office. Hag Harriet, the witch she talked about from home, apparently always wore hers. Grin wasn't sure if it was normal or even if Jess knew about it, but sometimes, when she was feeling very strongly about something, the atmosphere in the region of the point began to change. At the moment, heavy grey clouds were gathering, and a few large raindrops fell and landed on the brim, splashing gently.

He sighed, and put down his tools.

'Oh, come back,' he said. 'I'm sorry. I just felt a bit – oh, I don't know.'

'What?' she said, puzzled.

'Well, sort of upset. I mean, I thought we were good mates, but now you're saying you want to go off to some fancy school and – oh, you know ...' He shrugged.

Her face cleared. 'Oh, I *see*! But I'd write, and I'd come back and see you and everything! I'd miss you, I would really, but I do think I need to go. Anyway, you don't need to worry, because I probably won't win,' she said practically. 'I don't even know where to start. Here, look at the rules.' She spread the piece of paper out on the workbench, and they looked at it together.

'What do they mean by a theme?' she said doubtfully.

'Well, they always have a theme on *Changing Brooms*, don't they? Something like Moroccan Market Place or Municipal Rubbish Dump. What you need to do first is go to the shop and get some magazines about houses to get some ideas. You need to come up with something really unusual. Then you need to do plans; drawings. I can help you with that.'

'Right! I'll go now! And Grin ...'

'Yes?'

'Thanks!'

* * *

Jess went into the shop and bought some magazines with titles such as *Dream House* and *Modern Living*. Well, she didn't exactly buy them; she just fixed Mrs Raven with her serious deep blue eyes, and Mrs Raven found herself refusing to take any money for the magazines. She went back to the house and began to leaf through them. Soon, she became absorbed. There were pictures of all kinds of rooms in all kinds of houses. Some of them she hated, but there were lots that she could easily imagine living in.

Before long it was the middle of the afternoon. With a start, she realised she hadn't seen or heard Agnes since first thing. Usually by this time she would have had a whole list of jobs to do in the house, and Agnes would have asked her to cover at least two or three weatherwitching appointments as well. She made some tea and took it upstairs.

'Agnes?'

A sort of groan came from inside. Feeling very

slightly anxious, Jess called, 'Are you all right? Can I come in? I've brought you some tea.'

'Urrgghh,' said Agnes. Or it could possibly have been 'Mmmm'.

Jess tried the door but it wouldn't open, and then she remembered about the charm. 'You'll have to undo the charm, Agnes.'

A sulky voice muttered, 'Open, you stupid door. Please. Oh, all right, pretty please with glittery sequins on.' The door swung open.

Agnes sat slumped at the dressing table, with bags under her eyes big enough to take all the screwed up bits of paper which were littering the floor around her chair. Jess put the tea down.

'What's wrong, Agnes?' she said gently. 'You look terrible.'

'Oh, that's right! Throw it in my face! I know I look terrible! I always look terrible.'

'Well, yes, but ...'

That didn't seem to help much. Agnes howled, 'So I do! I knew it! All I wanted ...' Her voice was submerged by sniffles and hiccups. '... of something ...'

Jess backed away hastily. There seemed to be a serious possibility of getting unpleasantly damp.

'There, there,' she said uncertainly, 'there, there. Would – would you like me to get Sybil?'

'No! No, she mustn't know. She'll just laugh at me.' She peered at Jess, her eyes red; her hair looking like an electrified haystack. 'I suppose you're laughing at me too,' she said suspiciously.

'Oh no,' declared Jess, 'definitely not. I really wouldn't.'

Agnes seemed reassured. She looked round, as if to check that no one was listening, then beckoned Jess closer.

'You see,' she said, 'the truth is – promise you won't tell?'

'Absolutely,' said Jess, crossing all of her fingers. (She had more than most – she'd been born with an extra one on each hand. Hag Harriet had been very interested when she'd heard that; she'd gone round straight away to see baby Jess, and informed her astonished parents that they could well have a future witch on their hands – only the very best, including herself, she told them, had six fingers.)

'The truth is, I'm entering that competition. The *Changing Brooms* one. It could be my big chance! But the trouble is—' She began to look frantic again. '—the trouble is, I just can't do it! I don't know where to start!'

'There, there,' said Jess again hastily, as the demented expression began to reappear. 'Shall I fetch Sybil? Perhaps she could help.'

As soon as she'd said it, she realised that Sybil

was hardly likely to want to help Agnes when she was entering herself. But it didn't matter, because the same thought had occurred to Agnes.

'No! No, no, no, no, no, no, no! Because I think—' She clutched Jess's arm. '—I think that Sybil will enter it too. She went very quiet after we heard about it, and I happen to know – well, never mind what I know. But I think she'll go in for it. And she's good at all this stuff. So what I want you to do is just to go round to her place – and – well, have a little look. See what she's up to. You know, just a little peep. No harm in that, is there?'

'You mean,' said Jess, 'you want me to spy? And help you cheat?'

'No! No, nothing like that! I just need – a little nudge, that's all. Just a tiny little nudge. A nudgelet. A nudgikin.'

Agnes trying to be sweet was a truly horrible sight.

'I'll think about it,' said Jess.

'Well, don't think about it for too long,' said Agnes, sharply changing tack.

Jess marched downstairs, furious.

'What's the problem?'

It was Mulrooney, Sybil's cat, who had somehow found his way in and was curled up on a chair in the kitchen. For some reason that he would never explain, he only ever talked to Jess. This had seemed very flattering till she discovered how extremely annoying he could be, so the fun had quickly worn off. Jess now told him what had happened.

'So she wants me to spy for her! To help her! Can you believe it?'

'Ah,' said Mulrooney.

'What do you mean, "Ah"?'

'As Confucius may well have said, "The path may be hidden, but the way is clear."'

Jess snatched up a twig from the log basket and pointed it at Mulrooney.

'See this?' she said. 'This isn't a twig any more, it's a wand. Do you believe me?'

The twig was trembling, and blue sparks were flying from its tip.

'I believe you,' said Mulrooney, very quickly.

'Good. Because I don't know what it can do. And if you don't do some straight talking, right now, you're going to be the one who'll find out. Do I make myself clear?'

'You do. Yes. Very.'

'Right. So if you have an idea, spill it. And if you haven't, go and use up space in someone else's kitchen.'

'If you could see your way to putting it down – or just pointing it somewhere else ...'

Jess tossed the twig into the basket.

Mulrooney cleared his throat. 'Right. It's simple, really. You don't need to actually do any spying. You just make something stupid up for Agnes. Then she'll think you've helped her – though actually, of course, you won't have.'

Jess considered. It seemed to make sense. 'Yes, I see what you mean.'

'Really,' purred Mulrooney, 'thanks are just so unnecessary.'

'Good,' said Jess sweetly, 'then I won't be bothering with any.'

* * *

Jess took the magazines back to Grin's and was just showing him some of the rooms she liked when Mulrooney jumped gracefully in through the open window, landing neatly on top of them.

'Oh, for goodness' sake,' said Jess, 'can't you be more careful?'

'So sorry,' replied Mulrooney insincerely. 'All this work, everyone so busy – you should see how much Sybil's done! Really, it makes me feel quite tired. I think I shall have to settle down for a little snooze.' And he jumped down from the workbench and headed over to a comfortable looking pile of wood shavings.

'Oh no you don't,' said Jess, scooping him up. 'At least not before you tell me about Sybil.'

'What do you want to know?'

'Well,' said Jess, 'no details. That wouldn't be fair. But – how far has she got?'

'She's decided which room to use. And she must have—'

'Oh no!' Jess's hand flew to her mouth.

'What's up? What's going on?' asked Grin, who could only hear what Jess was saying and was beginning to think she'd gone mad.

'He talks – didn't I tell you? Can't you hear him? But anyway, never mind that – it's a disaster! Why didn't I think of it before? You have to use a room in your own house for the makeover, and I don't have one! It's no use – that's it, it's over!'

* * *

Half an hour later, Jess had given up looking tragic and was merely gloomy. Grin had suggested asking Sybil (Jess didn't think that was fair) and Agnes (Jess had just looked at him) and had even gone to ask his mother if she could use a room in their house. She had been very apologetic and said she really wished she could help but she was very happy with her house as it was, thank you. The truth was, she watched *Changing Brooms* too, and she'd seen some of the things that happened when witches got a bit over-enthusiastic and wasn't prepared to risk it.

Mulrooney had gone to sleep, Grin was fiddling with his carving, and Jess was idly doodling. She started off with the moon, and then she put some stars around it. Then she drew an owl flying across the sky and put some trees in further down. She liked drawing trees. She divided the trunks into branches, then the large branches into smaller branches, then the smaller branches into twigs. Where the branches of one tree met those of another, they formed arching patterns, networks of curves. She drew more.

'So what's this? You've given up on a room and you're designing a cathedral?' asked Grin, looking over her shoulder.

'What do you mean?'

'What you've drawn there – it looks like the roof of a cathedral.'

'No – it's trees.'

'Trees. Oh, yes, I see – of course it is.' He stared at the drawing. Mulrooney woke up, stretched, and came over to see what they were looking at.

'Ah,' he said, 'a green thought in a green shade.'

'Eh?' said Jess.

'What did he say?' asked Grin. She told him. Thoughtfully, he picked up her pencil and began to make some sketches.

'I think I may have an idea,' he said. But he

wouldn't tell her what it was, or even show her the sketches.

'No. You'll have to wait and see. I need to talk to Dad about it. You go home, and I'll come round in a bit – won't be long.' And he rushed out.

Jess remembered that she was supposed to be spying for Agnes, and that she had to think of something to tell her.

'Agnes,' she called through the door.

'You can come in. It's open. I stopped bothering with the charm. Don't see why I should be polite to a stupid door.'

'Film Star Bedroom,' said Jess, eying Agnes's red-circled eyes, ancient clothes, and untidy bedroom. 'That's Sybil's idea. It's all about glamour, you see.'

'*Glamour!* Sybil? She's about as glamorous as a knitted tea cosy! Whereas I …' Agnes looked immensely and extraordinarily pleased with herself. 'Thank you, Jessica,' she said graciously. 'I think I can safely say I'm on my way. I shan't forget this.'

As the door closed behind her, Mulrooney appeared.

'Laughing Boy's ready for you,' he said. 'Seems very pleased with himself. You'd better come and see.'

Chapter Five

'So what do you think?' asked Grin anxiously half an hour later. 'Do you like it? You don't think it's silly, do you?'

Jess studied the picture carefully. It was a quick sketch, which showed a very upmarket hut with a thatched roof. The uprights were four tree trunks, one at each corner. The front wall was partly open, and curving branches, which gave the effect of two heavy curtains which were caught back on either side, formed the entrance. Trees were sketched all round it.

A glow appeared round the top of Jess's hat. It was like the light you sometimes see on a special summer evening, when it's been raining but the clouds have rolled back, and everything's washed in a rich, sparkling golden light.

'Is that really going to be my room?' she asked.

'Yes. We could start work on it straight away, so it'll be ready for when you get through.'

'But what if I don't?' she asked. The golden

41

light began to dim. 'Then it'd be just a waste, wouldn't it?'

'No, it wouldn't be a waste. For one thing, you'd have your own room, your own place away from Agnes. And the other thing is, Dad says it would be like a showroom for us; it'd show people the kind of work we can do.'

'But isn't the competition just for witches?' she asked, puzzled.

'Yes, but I'm talking about after the competition. The room will still be there then, won't it? And everyone'll know about it because you'll have won the competition and been on television. But anyway, you *are* going to get through, aren't you? And not just that, you're going to win!'

'Yes,' said Jess firmly. 'You're absolutely right. Of course I am. No problem at all. Er – how do I start?'

The first task was to decide what the room was for. That was easy. It was going to be a study. Even if she managed to get a place at the Collegium, she wouldn't be able to go for a few months. She knew that there were large gaps in her knowledge of the theory of witchcraft. She could use the study to catch up, as well as to get away from Agnes, which would be even more of a good thing if she did happen to win. Jess shuddered as she thought about what life would be like with Agnes if that happened. It really didn't bear thinking about.

So the room needed a desk and bookshelves and somewhere comfortable to sit. And because she would be studying witchcraft, there was the obvious theme. The added advantage was that she knew about witchcraft, so she wouldn't have to do much research, whereas if she were trying to re-create something like a Moroccan bazaar, or a French chateau, she wouldn't know where to start.

Agnes was much too busy working on her own entry to have any time to spare for weatherwitchery. But fortunately it was May, which tended to be quiet anyway – even farmers couldn't usually find much to complain about.

So Jess had plenty of time to get on with her entry. There was a great deal to think about. There were all the obvious necessities, of course: furniture, lighting, flooring and walls. But the best bit was planning how to use her three shots of magic. Of course, she could just use it for practical purposes, like moving heavy beams of wood or laying floors. But it would be far more fun to use it to make things happen: interesting things, beautiful things, fantastical things ... She had plenty of ideas; it was just a question of which to choose.

It took all of the few days she had but

eventually it was ready. Jess had done a ground plan, showing where everything would go, and she'd done a series of sketches to illustrate some of the details. The last date she could post it to be sure of it reaching *Changing Brooms* in time was the fifth. That morning, she put everything in a large envelope and took it down to the village shop, which was also the post office.

Mrs Raven looked very interested when she saw the address. 'Oh!' she said. 'Another one! First Madam Parsons, then Madam Moonthistle and now you!' She peered through the wire grille at Jess in a way Jess really didn't like at all. What if she told Agnes that Jess had entered? She wouldn't put it past her – Mrs Raven loved to gossip, and being a shopkeeper and postmistress gave her lots of opportunities.

Jess thought quickly. Before she left Crumpet Thrubwell, Hag Harriet had given her a book called *The Complete Guide to Witchcraft*. She'd said she'd known Agnes and Sybil years before, when they were at school. 'They were always a few bristles short of a broomstick,' she'd said. 'This'll give you a bit of back-up.' Jess hadn't read all of it, but she had read the section on spells. She concentrated, picturing the page she needed. That was it! She raised her arm and pointed her finger at Mrs Raven.

'Nil memorandum!' she said clearly.

Mrs Raven looked startled. 'What was that, dear?' Then she looked puzzled. 'What was I saying?'

'Oh, nothing important,' smiled Jess.

She was a little worried over the next few days, as people complained about how the shop was running out of things because Mrs Raven kept forgetting to re-order – but soon everything was back to normal.

* * *

Then, for two weeks, there was nothing much to do except wait. Grin was busy working on the tree room with his father. Agnes spent a lot of time in her room; when she emerged, all she could talk about was how wonderful it would be to appear on television. She did no work, and didn't seem to care about whether or not Jess did either.

So there was a lot of time for Jess to spend wondering about whether or not she would make it into the final fifteen – and whether she really had a chance of going to the Collegium. It was odd, she sometimes thought. Only a few weeks before the idea had never entered her head, and yet now it seemed to fill it. She could picture herself there so easily: busy and happy, with lots of friends, working hard but still having fun … and her parents and Hag Harriet would be so proud.

But as the twenty-first of June drew closer, she began to feel more than a little nervous. As usual, they were all going to watch *Changing Brooms* at Sybil's house. But it was not going to be a normal evening. Sybil knew that she herself had entered, Agnes knew that she and Sybil had entered – but only Jess knew that all three of them had. Sybil would be surprised. But Agnes would feel betrayed. Jess had no delusions about that.

* * *

None of them really concentrated on the main part of the programme. Sybil kept jumping up and going into the kitchen to fetch drinks and nibbles. Agnes sat on the edge of her seat and didn't appear to hear anything anyone said to her. Jess looked through magazines as she usually did, but without taking anything in. She glanced at the others from time to time: it was obvious that they really cared about the competition. For the first time, Jess wondered why. She knew why she cared; she needed the money for the Collegium. But what was in it for Sybil and Agnes? Why were they so desperate for ten thousand pounds?

Tiffany Taylor's voice interrupted her musings, and she sat up sharply as she realised that the moment had come.

'Well, of course, you're all absolutely dying to know which of you brilliant would-be designers out there are going to have the chance to appear on our special competition programme. I know I am,' declared Tiffany.

'I have the winning names here, in this envelope ...' She twinkled as she held it up. 'And I'm going to ask Lancelot to come and read them out. Come on, Lance!'

'Sweetie, I thought you'd never ask!' Lancelot's dark brown eyes gleamed, first towards Sylvia, then at the camera, as his long, elegant fingers opened the envelope and extracted the piece of paper inside.

'I promise you,' confided Lance, 'I have absolutely no idea who the winners are. Bizarrely enough, the producers failed to ask me to be on the judging panel – can you believe it darling? I certainly couldn't … Anyway, let's see. Here we go!'

He read through twelve names. The tension in the room was electric. Then he paused.

'And something very surprising here. The last three finalists all come from the same village – would you believe it? It must be something in the air. Anyway, their names are: Agnes Moonthistle, Sybil Parsons and Jessica Fraser. Well done to you!'

He turned to Tiffany. 'Well, Tiffany, that'll save the producers a few bob, won't it? They'll be able to get away with one adjudicator for all three of them. Be a bit hectic, won't it?'

'Yes, Lance, it certainly will!' beamed Tiffany merrily. 'It'll keep him jolly busy, won't it, Lance?'

Lancelot looked at her. 'Do tell, Tiffany. Who's it going to be? I have a distinctly bad feeling about this ...'

Tiffany turned to the camera. 'Well, there we have it, viewers! I'm off on holiday, and Lance will soon be off to Melton Magna! The programme's away now till June, but we'll be back with our special extended competition edition on Midsummer's Eve. See you all then – bye for now!' The jolly *Changing Brooms* theme began, and Sybil switched the television off.

There was silence. It was not a good silence. Agnes looked at Jess, Jess looked at Agnes and Sybil looked at both of them. For a precious minute, no one could think of a word to say. But that was too good to last. Finally, Agnes stirred, and levelled a gaze that had splinters of ice in it towards Jess.

'Viper!' she hissed. 'Traitor!'

Sybil looked anxious and confused. 'What's the matter, Agnes? Why are you looking at Jess like that?'

'Didn't you *hear*? Don't you *understand*? She knew I was going in for that competition – she knew how much it meant to me! And yet she's gone behind my back and put in an entry of her own!'

'But I entered too. Are you cross with me as well?'

'Oh, don't be silly. I knew you'd gone in for it.'

'You did?' Sybil looked astonished. 'But how? I kept it secret – I thought you'd think I was being silly. So how did you find out? And why didn't you say anything?'

'Because I didn't want to embarrass you!' she said. 'But *her* – I thought she was helping me, but all the time – I bet you were actually spying on me, weren't you? I can't believe it – I take you into my own home, treat you like a daughter, and this is the thanks I get! Well – take that!'

She drew herself up dramatically and lightning zigzagged from her fingertips and shot towards Jess. But Jess was just as good a weatherwitch as Agnes, if not better. She quickly held up her own hand. The lightning turned into a black cloud which whizzed back until it was above Agnes's head, where it promptly released a downpour. Agnes was drenched. Furious, she declared: 'You are no longer welcome in my house! I shall write to those miserable parents of yours and tell them so!'

Then, sneezing, squelching, and dripping steadily on to the carpet, she stalked out.

Sybil looked round at her decidedly damp living room. 'Oh dear,' she said.

'Oh Sybil,' said Jess, 'I'm so sorry. I didn't mean to make such a mess.'

'Don't give it a thought, dear. This is the room that's going to have the makeover, anyway. I've had enough of all these flowers and flounces. But I think perhaps you have a bit of explaining to do ...'

* * *

'… And so that's how it all happened,' finished Jess. 'For me, it's a way to get to the Collegium Witchorum. But I'm really, truly sorry I tried to spy on you. I wasn't trying to copy your ideas. I just thought I might get some idea about how to start.'

'You should have asked,' said Sybil gently. 'I would have helped you. Anyway, you found your own way, didn't you? With a little help from your friends.'

'Yes,' said Jess, 'you're right, I did. But Sybil, if you don't mind me asking – why did you enter?'

'Oh, for the money, of course. But if you don't mind, I'm not going to tell you what I want it for. That can wait – if I win, I'll tell you then. But you know, we're forgetting the most important thing.'

'What's that?'

'We're through! We're both through to the next round! We've done really well, and with a lot of work, and a good dusting of magic, one of us might do even better. So come on – let's celebrate – I know you're very young, and your parents might not approve, but I think this calls for champagne!'

Jess went into the kitchen to fetch some glasses. Mulrooney was comfortably curled up on his favourite chair. He opened one eye.

'Ah,' he said. 'The cabaret.'

'The what?'

'The sideshow, *Broomfight at the OK Corral*. The best show since *Macbeth*. Never heard of that either? "In thunder, lightning, or in rain; When shall we three meet again?" No? Oh, I just don't know what they teach you young people nowadays.'

'We didn't use brooms, silly. They're for riding on, not fighting with.'

'Poetic licence. Have you no soul?'

She looked at him curiously. 'You're very strange, you know. Exactly what kind of a cat are you, anyway?'

He stretched. 'Oh, you know. The purrfect kind. Remember to put a bit of champagne in my bowl, won't you?'

Chapter Six

Mill Farm
Crumpet Thrubwell

26 May

Dear Daughter,

I am writing in haste because I have just had a very strange letter from Cousin Agnes. She says some very unpleasant things about you which I know cannot be true, but most of all I am worried because she says you are no longer living with her. Please let me know by return what is going on – I am feeling very anxious.

I was going to write anyway because I heard your name mentioned on Changing Brooms. I didn't think you particularly liked it – you always laugh at me when I watch it! Are you really in the competition? I wonder if you'll meet that lovely Lancelot Marchpane – perhaps you could get a signed photograph if you do. I hope to hear from you soon.

Love,
Mother

6 The Barrows
Melton Magna

30 May

Dear Mum,

Please don't worry about me. Agnes is cross because she didn't know I had entered the Changing Brooms competition, and she thinks I should have told her - she entered it as well, you see.

Perhaps it's all for the best. I never told you before, because I know how difficult it is for you to afford the money you give to Agnes for teaching me - but she really isn't very good as a teacher, and I'm afraid she's not a very nice person either. I'm not just making excuses. I'm living with Sybil - Madam Parsons, now. I've told you about her, she's Agnes's friend. Well, she was - I'm not sure if they're still fiends now. Anyway, she's a very nice person, and she's going to write to you as well to explain all about it.

It's very exciting about the competition. We have another week to get ready, and then the Changing Brooms team - with Lancelot Marchpane! - will be coming down to film all three of us in turn as we do the makeover. They film everybody, but of course they'll edit it so that you'll only see bits about each finalist's room in the finished programme.

My friend Grin and his father, who are woodworkers, are building me a sort of very fancy hut – I suppose you could call it a tree house – for me to use for my room. Sybil says I could have used a room in her house, but I didn't realise that at the time, and anyway, I really like the tree house.

The other thing I should tell you is that if I win, I thought I would use the money so that I could go to the Collegium Witchorum. I hope you think this is a good idea. It would mean that in the future I should be able to earn a lot of money and would be able to help you and Dad and the little ones (but not Joe, he can look after himself!)

Much love,

Jess

Mill Farm
Crumpet Thrubwell

5 June

My dear Jess,

We are all very proud of you. You seem to be doing very well, and most importantly, it sounds as if you have made some very good friends. I had a lovely letter from Madam Parsons. I shall give Cousin Agnes a piece of my mind when I see her, believe you me – mind you, they always were a bit funny on that side of the family.

Goodness me, what a thing it would be if you went to the College. Well, we shall have to wait and see. Good luck with the filming, I hope all goes well. We are all looking forward to seeing the programme. Not long now, is it?

Much love,

Mother

Practically everyone turned out to greet the *Changing Brooms* team when they rolled into town. Most people had a personal, financial interest – they'd placed bets on one or more of the witches, and there'd been much discussion about their chances. Sybil was the favourite; they reckoned that she had a much better idea about what looked good than Agnes, who had certainly shown no sign of being interested in such things up till now. On the other hand, Agnes had a strong personality, and might just pull off something quirky that would appeal to the viewers. Jess was very much an outsider – after all, she was so much younger. But then that made for good odds – if she did win, anyone who'd placed a bet on her stood to make a lot of money.

Mrs Raven was looking forward to making lots of money selling snacks and drinks, and everyone was keen to rub shoulders with people they'd seen on TV. Maybe, they'd even appear on screen themselves, if they could manage to stroll casually into shot at the right moment.

The makeovers were to be done and filmed one after the other – Sybil first, then Agnes, and finally Jess. Lancelot – 'Call me Lance, darlings!' – explained that this was because they only had one film crew – the programme had two, but time was very tight because there were so many people to be filmed, and the other crew was busy elsewhere.

Filming had to take place in conditions of the strictest security. 'Can't have you being tempted to nick ideas from each other, can we dears? And do be careful where you direct your magic. We don't want any nasty accidents, now do we?'

All this was being explained at a planning meeting, which was being held at Sybil's house. Agnes had offered hers, but Lance had taken one look at the state of the kitchen and politely declined.

'I'll be around to lend a hand or an ear and you're also allowed an assistant – you can choose your own, or you can borrow ours, Clever Trevor. Which is it to be?'

Sybil and Agnes both opted for Trevor, but Jess said she'd rather have Grin, if that was all right.

'Grim? Oh, *Grin*! What a perfectly splendid name! After Grinling Gibbons? Ah, the world famous woodcarver who did lots of stuff at Chatsworth? Fabulous! Of course you can have

Grin. I shall look forward to meeting him.'

It was the first time Sybil and Jess had met Agnes since the night of the Broomfight. Agnes seemed to be torn between being nasty to them and smarmy with Lance and the crew. She was looking rather startling. Her hair had been cut and streaked, and instead of glasses she had coloured contact lenses, so that her eyes were a brilliant emerald green. She had lots of make-up on and new, sharply-cut clothes.

'She's really into makeovers, isn't she?' whispered Jess to Sybil. Lance edged away nervously when she got too close.

'Formidable lady, your friend, isn't she?' he murmured to Sybil.

'Indeed she is,' replied Sybil diplomatically, 'indeed she is.'

There were some rather strange incidents during filming. First, all Sybil's tins of paint mysteriously changed colour overnight. Then the whole crew was set on by a plague of jumbo-sized mosquitoes. Finally, and worst of all, Clever Trevor noticed that his fingers had all turned into thumbs. Understandably, he found this very distressing and threatened to quit. Fortunately, there was a consultant witch on hand in case of just such eventualities, and she soon had everything sorted out.

'She was very good,' Sybil told Jess. 'She knew straight away what to do. She said people get up to the strangest tricks when they're really desperate to win. I'm afraid she was suggesting that you or Agnes might have been behind it all. Well, obviously you wouldn't be, and I'd hate to think that even Agnes would go that far ...'

But strangely enough, nothing happened when it was Agnes's turn to be filmed. After that, the witch had quietly put a spell of protection round the tree house, so although freak weather conditions and other strange occurrences were observed in the vicinity, filming was uninterrupted.

Within a week, it was all over. It had been exhausting. Jess had never, ever worked as hard. She'd had help, of course, from Grin and from Lance, who'd made some very helpful suggestions, and she and Grin had actually done a lot of the work beforehand – but even so, the pressure had been intense.

But now the rooms had all been sealed off till after the results had been announced, and there was nothing left to do but wait, till the twenty-first of June.

6 The Barrows
Melton Magna

16 June

Dear all,

Well, the filming's over, and I don't know whether I'm glad or sorry – it was really hard work, but it was brilliant!

I was worried that Grin and his dad wouldn't be able to get the tree house finished in time before the Changing Brooms crew arrived. I helped as much as I could, but there wasn't a huge amount I could do – they were the experts. Anyway, they did it, and they made a fantastic job of it. Then I just had to do my bit.

It seemed really odd at first, having a camera man following me round. But it's funny, after a bit you just don't notice it. I'm not going to tell you how I did the room – it would take too long, and anyway you'll see it soon on the programme – but I hope you'll like it. I was really pleased with the way it looked in the end.

Lancelot was really nice, Mum. I thought he might be a bit of a show off, or snooty or something, but he wasn't at all – he gave us loads of tips about how to do things, and he had some really good ideas. I suppose he shouldn't have suggested stuff really, but I think he liked what we were doing and he just got a bit carried away. He gave me a lovely signed photograph for you, which I'm sending with this letter.

Not long now – I can't wait till the 21st. Keep your fingers crossed for me!

Cheers for now – I hope everything's all right? I've just realised it's a while since I heard from you.

Take care,
Much love,

Jess

Chapter Eight

At last, the day came. The entire village had decided that there were two excellent excuses for a party – it was Midsummer's Eve, and three of their own were going to be on television.

Sybil and Jess had helped to set things up: Sybil had set tiny lights throughout the trees on the village green, without the bother of electrical wires, and Jess had done her best with the weather: unfortunately the moon wasn't full – there were limits as to what she could achieve – but she had sent a front of rain clouds racing smartly in the opposite direction when they threatened to spoil the fun, so it was going to be a clear and lovely evening.

A big screen had been set up in The Rest and Be Thankful pub, and there was another one on the green itself, but Sybil and Jess felt that they needed to be away from all of that, so they had decided to watch the programme at Sybil's.

Just as they were nervously settling into their seats in the kitchen – they were not able to use the living room yet, of course – every door in the house crashed violently open, and then banged just as noisily shut. Lights flashed on and off, the radio and CD player switched themselves on and off, and the table, looking terrified, went for a walk and tried to hide in a corner, followed swiftly by the chairs. In the middle of all the mayhem, and almost unnoticed, there was a heavy thump as something landed on the floor. Into the silence that followed walked a tall woman wearing a black velvet cloak trimmed with sequins and a matching pointed hat. She propped her broomstick beside the door.

'Thought I'd just drop in and join the fun,' she said, smiling cheerfully. 'Goodness, is this all because of me? What a kerfuffle.' She snapped her fingers and the chairs and table scuttled obediently back into place. She took off the cloak and sighed with relief. 'Thank goodness for that. I was boiling, but you have to look the part, don't you? Standards have to be maintained – wouldn't you agree, Agnes?' She looked round absently. 'Now, where did I put her down?'

The heap on the floor stirred and groaned.

'Harriet!' gasped Jess. 'But *how*?'

'Oh, never mind the whys and the wherefores. Mulrooney, good to see you.'

Mulrooney leapt up onto Harriet's knee and curled up, purring and looking very much at home.

'How – how dare you?' spluttered Agnes, picking herself off the floor,

'Ah, feeling better?' enquired Harriet, looking round for somewhere to sit. 'Jolly good. Thought you'd like to drop in. You always watch the programme together, don't you? What fun. Do you remember those happy days we all used to have together at school? We really must catch up later. Anyway, must be time for the programme to start – come on, let's all get comfortable!'

Not bothering to look for the remote control, she pointed at the television and Tiffany Taylor's face appeared on the screen, just as the merry lilt of the *Changing Brooms* theme tune faded away.

'Good evening and welcome,' Tiffany said to the camera, 'to our very special Midsummer's Eve edition of *Changing Brooms*. Tonight we're going to find out how the contestants in our fabulous "Room for a Broom" competition got on when they were given the chance to turn their dreams into reality. And then you're going to vote on who made the best job of it; more details about how to do that at the end of the programme.

'If you remember, the challenge was to transform a room of their own in the usual two days. And I can promise you, they came up with some pretty unusual rooms, and some very imaginative transformations! We're starting up in Scotland, and then we'll move steadily south. Each area had either myself or Lance to keep an eye on things.

'First of all, we talked to the contestants about what they were trying to achieve. So here we go, on the beginning of a long – and sometimes very strange – journey through the British Isles. We'll begin in Bonnie Scotland, and believe me, this will give us a very spooky start to the evening!

'Jean MacPherson persuaded the owner of her local castle to let her transform a little-used dungeon into a very characterful teashop! Now here she is, telling us how she plans to do it!'

A shot of a cheery looking woman warmly wrapped up in masses of tartan and woolly scarves appeared in front of a bleak and windswept castle, with a bit of brooding moor in the background.

'Oh, hullo, Tiffany – would you care to borrow one of my scarves? It does get a little nippy up here, doesn't it? Especially round this particular castle. Yes, that's right, there was a particularly nasty massacre near here in the seventeenth century, and the area's had a bit of a reputation ever since. We don't tend to get many tourists, but I thought a nice wee teashop could make all the difference – so why don't you come away in and see the dungeon?'

The viewers then saw Tiffany's face, lit by a swaying lantern, peering enthusiastically into the dark.

'Wow, this is terrific! What a sensationally gloomy dungeon! And what do you plan to do with it, Jean?'

Jean MacPherson beamed. 'Well, I thought I'd play to its strengths with a Gothic theme. We still have the old rack there, and that's going to make a lovely table. Look, can you see the blood stains? Fabulous, aren't they? And those skeletons there – well, let me give you a wee taster of what I'm going to do with them.'

There was a heap of old bones lying in a corner. Jean smiled encouragingly in their direction, and said brightly, 'Come on now! Hoots, toots, and awae ye go!'

The bones began to twitch. Then they clattered into two separate piles, as if they were attached to strings pulled by an invisible puppet master. Next, they began to link up: foot bones to leg bones, leg bones to hip bones, and so on, just like in the song. In no time at all, two complete skeletons stood to attention. Jean nodded her head, looking pleased.

'Well done! Now – just one more thing …' she pointed a finger, and on each one appeared a natty little tartan pinafore and a matching cap. 'Lovely, girls!' she said proudly, and turned to Sylvia. 'Don't they look just the ticket?'

The skeletons looked very deeply unhappy. There was an unmistakeable air of menace in the way their sightless skulls glared at Jean. One of them reached up with its bony fingers, took off its cap and crumpled it, slowly.

Tiffany, looking pale, said, 'Well, you're obviously raring to go, and who am I to get in the way? I'll just – go off and leave you to it with Clever Trevor. Good luck, guys!'

Sybil was spellbound. 'Goodness! It makes my room seem really dull! I hope there aren't many more like that!'

Agnes snorted, 'I read about that one in the preview in the paper. It said the ghosts in the dungeon took offence at being disturbed. It didn't end well.'

They watched a little longer. Sybil winced. 'Oh yes. Oh dear.'

Harriet shook her head. 'Never a good idea to mix spooks and sorcery. Always causes trouble.'

The next few were much more ordinary. Then it was the turn of the north-east.

'Oh, look!' said Harriet. 'Isn't that old Cushy Butterfield? Don't you remember her, from school? Very nice girl. Went up to Tyneside to be a sea witch, but of course all the shipyards have closed down now, so I expect she could do with the cash. Now what's she up to?'

Cushy, it turned out, owned a little terraced miner's house which still had the old outside loo out at the back.

'I want to turn it into a summer-house, Tiffany,' she explained. 'I know it's a bit of a challenge, but I'm sure I can do it. I'll retain as many of the original features as possible, of course.'

Tiffany turned to the camera and pulled a face. 'Not too many, I hope!'

And so the programme went on. Jess's favourite was a witch from the south-east called Malcolm. Lance was shown interviewing him at the end of his project, rather than at the beginning.

'So, Malcolm,' said Lance, 'Tell us about this – er – room.'

'It's a garden room, Lance,' said Malcolm, sounding rather mournful.

Lance looked round enthusiastically.

'Um – I've got to say, Malcolm old mate, it looks just like a garden to me.' He looked more closely at the borders. 'A black garden, actually.'

He looked at the camera, and confided, 'No kidding – all the flowers are black!'

'That's right, Lance. I've got black grass, black tulips, black pansies, black hollyhocks – you name it, I've got it. In black.'

Lance was looking slightly desperate. 'And where did the magic come in?'

'Black magic, Lance. It's a completely new concept, you see. Outside meets inside. It's a reflection of the void inside us all.'

'Very interesting, Malcolm. Well, moving swiftly on …' He threw an aside to the camera. 'How on earth did that one get through? Now if I'd been on the judging panel …'

At last, they came to the final area – the south-west. Jess, Sybil, Harriet and even Agnes had been laughing and exchanging comments about the other entries, but now the tension quickly rose again.

Jess tried to breathe deeply and calmly. So far, she hadn't seen anything that seemed obviously better than the tree-house – though she knew it was impossible to predict the verdict of the viewers. But she really had no idea what Sybil or Agnes's rooms would be like. Agnes had certainly looked very pleased with herself after she'd finished her room. And in fact she looked remarkably calm and confident now, even after her undignified entrance. In fact, she looked almost as if she knew something that the others didn't. Jess was puzzled. But then her attention was diverted. Lance was on the screen again, talking to Sybil.

'So, Sybil, tell me about the room you've chosen and what you hope to do with it.'

'Well, Lance,' said Sybil nervously, 'I've chosen my living room. I decorated it some years ago and I liked it then. But – well, I feel I'm ready for a change.'

'Ah! So we're looking for something exciting and cutting edge, are we?'

'Not exactly, no. What I wanted was a room that looked up to the minute and fresh, but would also be really comfortable to actually spend time in. I've called it "a simple room".'

Lance looked interested. 'Well now, there's an extremely novel idea! I'm looking forward to this. OK, Sybil, I'll leave you to it.'

The next shot was of Lance walking down Grin's garden.

'Now this is really different!' he said, brushing some specks of mud from his leather trousers. 'Come on, young Jess – tell us all about it!'

'Well,' said Jess, 'I didn't have a room, so a friend of mine built this for me.' She leaned towards the camera and confided, 'He's an apprentice with his dad, and they're starting up a firm called Creative Carpentry, and they're very good – and very reasonable!'

'Fantastic!' marvelled Lance. 'And what's the room for, Jess?'

'It's a study,' said Jess. 'You see, I'm an apprentice too, but of course I'm an apprentice witch. I'd really like to be able to go to the Collegioum Witchorum to study, but – well, it costs too much money. So I wanted a room that would help me study by myself. And I thought that if I made witchcraft the theme, it'd be kind of an inspiration.'

Lance opened his eyes wide. 'Wow! Serious stuff! See you soon, Jess, and good luck!'

In the next shot, Lance was standing outside Agnes's hovel. 'Hm,' he said. 'Well, as you can see, Agnes's lovely home – as the estate agents say – has many original features. Come and meet her – she's quite a character.'

He led the camera up the stairs, where Agnes was waiting for him.

'This way, Lance,' she trilled, and she led the way into Jess's old bedroom.

'As you can see, Lance,' she said, 'this room is desperately in need of a makeover. Until recently, my apprentice was living here, and to be frank, she certainly wasn't the tidiest of girls!'

'No, I can see that,' agreed Lance.

'What I want is a complete change of image for the whole house.' She simpered coyly. 'I've had a bit of a change of image myself because to be honest with you, I want to make some changes in my life. In fact, I'm hoping that appearing on your little show will be the springboard for a new career – as a TV presenter!'

Lance looked startled. 'Oh! Well, I'm sure we all wish you the very best of luck with that. And what's your theme to be?'

She fluttered her eyelashes. Jess had never seen a sight quite like it. 'Oh, glamour, Lance. What else?'

Jess giggled. Harriet burst out laughing, and even kind Sybil smothered a smile. But Agnes didn't seem to care. 'You may mock,' she said grandly, 'but I'll have the last laugh. You just see if I don't.'

Jess leaned forward. Sybil's finished room was on screen. 'Oh, Sybil,' she said, 'it's lovely!'

Sybil's living room had been completely stripped of all its frills and flounces. The walls were pale and the floorboards had been sanded and polished. The chairs and settee had been re-covered in a plain soft blue and the fireplace now had a simple metal surround. In front of it was a large, soft rug, in shades of blue and green. The collection of crystal balls now hung in front of the window so that the sunlight shone through them, making soft rainbow patterns on the walls. The long curtains were made of some thin filmy material, scattered with butterflies, which moved their wings gently.

At the other end of the room was a table with a beautiful light hanging over it. The light was made of curved wires with a tiny lampshade, shaped like a tulip, at the end of each wire, which trembled slightly. As they watched, the tulip petals fell off one by one, melting into thin air as they drifted down. In their place, at the end of each wire a tiny rosebud appeared, which rapidly opened out into a flower. Several butterflies flew over from the curtains and alighted gently on the roses before flying back to their places.

'Tell us about how you used your magic, Sybil,' said Lance.

'The crystal balls just hang by themselves. I didn't want to have to bother with string or wire. It's a bit high maintenance, that one, I have to admit – I don't know how long they'd stay there without a top-up. Then the butterflies – oh, and the light. The flowers change according to season. I wanted to keep just a few flowers,' she said apologetically.

'And I'm sure everybody's glad you did! Well done, Sybil – brilliant!'

The next room was Agnes's, and it was very different. The walls were gold, there was a gilt and crystal chandelier, and the bed had a purple velvet cover embroidered with gold thread. There were satin cushions and lots of mirrors. It was completely over the top. Worst of all was a picture of the new-look Agnes hanging on one wall, which simpered and winked.

'Phew,' said Lance, 'What can I say?'

Agnes lounged across the bed. 'I know,' she smiled, 'I know. Personality. You've either got it or you haven't.'

Tiffany reappeared on the screen. 'Well, two very different rooms there. And now it's time for our last, and youngest contestant – Jessica Fraser. Let's have a look at what she did with her tree-house …'

Jess swallowed. She loved her room. But what would everyone else think? It mattered. It mattered a lot. She watched as the camera moved round the tree house, showing how it looked from every angle.

Between the branches which formed the uprights of the house were alcoves in each of which was a painting. One showed a cat, another a witch on a broomstick, another an owl, and so on. All the pictures moved: the owl swooped, flapping its wings with slow motion grace, the witch whizzed through the night sky, and the cat – which Jess noticed for the first time showed a remarkable resemblance to

Mulrooney – arched its back and stretched. On the ceiling, the moon and stars and planets slowly wheeled through space.

The only furniture, apart from bookshelves, was a desk and chair. The desk top was made out of a cross-section of wood from a great tree that had fallen some years before in a gale. The chair was made out of a partially hollowed tree trunk. There was a vase of wild flowers on the desk, and most of the front wall was glass, so that while you were working you could look out at the shifting patterns of the leaves.

'Isn't there something rather special about the books?' asked Lance. 'Could you show us?'

The Jess on television smiled and took down a book It was a history of witchcraft. She opened it up at a chapter on hedgewitches. A sleepy looking small witch, dressed all in brown, stepped out on to the desk.

'So you'd like to know about flying with the birds, would you?' she said. 'Well, it's a marvellous thing to do, but it can be very dangerous, and believe me, it wears you out!'

'Goodness!' said Sybil.

Harriet said nothing, but she leaned forward intently.

'Well, now you've seen all of the contestants,' Tiffany was saying, 'and it's decision time. These are the numbers to ring ...' She went through them. 'And the lines are open – now! We'll be back in three quarters of an hour!'

* * *

Jess couldn't bear it. She jumped up and said she was going out to see if she could find Grin.

The villagers were all hurrying home to vote. Those she passed smiled kindly at her and gave her the thumbs-up. She heard snatches of conversation, but tried not to listen; she didn't want to know what people thought, she just wanted to know the result.

On second thoughts, she slipped round the back of Grin's house, and went down to the tree house. Kind as they were, she didn't want to have to talk to his parents at the moment. She found that the room was open: the spell which had sealed it must have been timed to break when the programme was over. She went in, and touched the desk. The wood was smooth and golden; Grin had done a beautiful job. She hoped he and his father got lots of commissions as a result of all the publicity – she didn't know how else she could possibly thank them for all they'd done.

She looked at the pictures on the walls. The owl swooped close to the surface of the wall, as if it was looking through a window, and gazed at her seriously. She sensed that it was trying to comfort her. The witch flew by on her broomstick, took off her hat and waved it merrily. Even the cat gave an encouraging miaow.

'I thought I might find you here.' It was Harriet. 'It means a lot to you, doesn't it, winning this competition?'

'Yes, well, especially now. I don't know what I'll do if I can't go to the Collegium. I mean, I couldn't go back to Agnes's now – I wouldn't want to, even if she'd have me.'

'Oh, I don't think you need to worry too much,' said Harriet comfortably. 'Futures was never my strongest subject, but I'm not bad at it, and I've got a strong hunch that you'll end up at the Collegium.'

'Really?' Jess gazed at her hopefully.

'I can't be sure, but I think there's a very good chance of it. Good job, too, your parents could do with something to cheer them up – oh!' She clapped her hand to her mouth. 'Whoops.'

'What? What do you mean? Is something wrong at home?' Jess demanded.

'Well – I wasn't going to tell you yet, because I didn't want to spoil your evening. In fact, your mother made me promise I wouldn't say anything. Oh dear.'

'You've got to tell me now!'

'Yes, well, I'm afraid your Joe's been a bit silly. More than a bit silly this time. He decided he wanted to have a go at driving the tractor. So he did. Right into the side of the barn. And of course the insurance won't cover that – they say it's not an accident. You know how tight things are in farming these days – it's going to make things very difficult for them. But don't worry, they'll manage somehow, I'm sure they will,' she said hastily, seeing Jess's stricken face.

Grin appeared in the doorway. 'We saw you both coming down here – whatever are you doing? They're just about to announce the results – come on, you've not got time to go home, come and watch it with us.'

In a daze, Jess followed.

Chapter Nine

'So,' said Tiffany, 'the votes have all been registered and the lines are closed. Now, the contestants didn't know this was going to happen, but we've got our local television colleagues on standby, with a video link ready – and while we just remind you again of all the finished rooms, one of them's going to be rushing off to talk to the winner! Not much longer now!'

They saw almost all the rooms again. Jess kept jumping up and down to see if a camera crew was running up the path. 'I can't possibly have won,' she cried in despair. 'They'd be here by now if I had!'

No one knew what to say. Then suddenly, Grin leapt up. 'No, they wouldn't because they'd expect you to be at Sybil's!'

He ran to the door, yelling that he would go and see, but just as he got there and wrenched it open, an exhausted-looking young man appeared, swiftly followed by a cameraman.

'Jess Fraser?' panted the first one. 'Oh, thank

goodness for that! I'm not fit enough for this kind of thing! Right – ready? You're on air – now!'

Tiffany gazed out of the television screen. 'And the winner is – Jessica Fraser, our youngest contestant! The voting was really close, but she just made it by a cat's whisker! Congratulations! Now then, Jess. Just tell us again – what is it you're planning to do with the money?'

Jess was quiet for a moment. Then she looked steadily into the camera, and said, 'Thank you, Tiffany. As a matter of fact, there's been a bit of a change of plan. I've decided that – that the money's needed elsewhere. By my parents, actually – they've had some bad news. So I won't be going to the Collegium Witchorum after all. I – I can't really say anything else. I'm sorry.'

Tears were running down her cheeks. Everyone gazed at her, thunderstruck. Then Grin's mum jumped up and hugged her. Meanwhile Tiffany was looking bewildered, for once unsure what to say. But she didn't need to worry, because a woman none of them had ever seen before suddenly marched prposefully into shot and took the microphone from Tiffany.

'Excuse me, dear. Damaris Tremayne, head teacher at the Collegium. I was invited to be in the audience tonight, and I'm very glad I was. I must say, I very nearly didn't come – not my kind of thing at all – but I had a tip off from my old friend Hag Harriet that there was someone I ought to watch out for – and she was absolutely right!

'I'm not interested in interior design, not interested at all. But I am interested in young people – especially young people who want to be witches. And what I've seen tonight is a young lady who wants a place in my school, and who's shown beyond doubt that she deserves a place – on the grounds of both talent and determination.' She gazed directly into the camera. 'Is this right? Yes? Now listen to me,

Jessica Fraser. Money or no money, I would be delighted if you would come and take up a place at the Collegium. I've seldom seen such ability, nor such enthusiasm. So turn off the waterworks, and when you've finished celebrating, start working through all those books in your tree house – I presume they're not just for show? – and we'll see you in September. Well done!'

* * *

The partying went on for a long time. In the end, everyone was happy. Sybil received so many requests from potential clients that, as she assured Jess, she really didn't need the money to help her get set up, which was all she'd wanted it for. Agnes boasted that she'd already had a call from an agent who thought she'd be just right for a new game show called Gone In A Blink They wanted a witch with charisma to be the host, someone who would (temporarily) turn the losing contestants into something nasty, before booting them off the show. It sounded like a terrible idea to everyone else, but as far as she was concerned, she'd already got it, and it was going to be fantastic.

Lancelot Marchpane had been very impressed with the work of Grin and his father, and promised to use them in his work for private clients.

Jess decided that she needed to go home and see her family. Apart from anything else, she wanted to see for herself that everything was going to be all right. And she might just have a sisterly word or two with Joe. It really was about time he sorted himself out.

'Excellent,' declared Harriet, 'you can come back with me. As a matter of fact, I've got a couple of presents for you – it'll give you a chance to try one of them out.'

She rummaged about in the folds of her cloak and produced a small, narrow package. She'd obviously had trouble wrapping it up, but once Jess had managed to get through all the sellotape, she found a perfect miniature broom.

Harriet pointed at it. 'Maximise!' she ordered.

The broom instantly expanded into a full-sized one. It was strong and sturdy, with a comfortable seat and handlebars. Jess gasped.

'A new broom! It's wonderful! But – I've not had proper lessons. I don't think I could ride it all the way to Crumpet Thrubwell.'

'Nonsense,' said Harriet crisply. 'You'll soon learn. Piece of cake. Mulrooney'll help, won't you?'

'Me?' Mulrooney looked horrified. 'I'm not going on a broom with a learner driver!'

'Oh yes you are,' said Harriet cheerfully. 'Didn't I mention that you're the other present?

Jess will be needing a cat.'

Jess grinned at him. 'Come on then, Mulrooney. Welcome aboard.'

And soon, after a few wobbles and tumbles and some sharp words from Mulrooney, they were off.

about the author

Sue Purkiss was born in Ilkeston, in Derbyshire and studied English at Durham University – but before that, at the age of twelve, she knew that she could one day write a novel. A few years later, her first, *Spook School* was published by A & C Black in the Black Cats series, and launched Sue's career as a talented and original children's writer.

In the intervening years, Sue worked in London for a firm called FMT Writing Services and also worked as a teacher in Leicester and in Somerset. She undertook a writing course in Bristol and wrote short stories for adults as well as some work for educational publishers. Then she realized it would be more fun to write for children.

Today she lives in Cheddar and combines writing fiction with working on a young offenders programme in the Somerset area. *Changing Brooms* is her second novel, and she has plans for many more.

*About **Changing Brooms**, Sue Purkiss writes ...*

'Somerset, where I live, is a county that oozes magic. Glastonbury is full of it – every other shop sells crystals and other magical necessities. Then there's Wookey Hole, with its ancient tale of a very sinister witch indeed. But the inspiration for this story was the Witch House at Hestercombe Gardens, near Taunton. It's over three hundred years old, but has been recently restored – and it is the most enchanting place, with a thatched roof, chairs carved out of a single piece of wood, driftwood sculptures that look like mythical beasts, and silhouettes of witchy things on the walls.

'I think that was the start of it. Well, that, and a certain TV programme ...'

Another fantastic Black Cat ...

SUE PURKISS
Spook School

What could be worse for a ghost than
not being spooky enough? That's
Spooker's problem as he faced his
all-important Practical Haunting exam.
It doesn't help that his task is to haunt
a brand-new house – hardly the kind
of dark, dingy place where ghosts
are meant to dwell!

But when Spooker makes a new friend,
he might just find a solution to
his problems …

Another fantastic Black Cat ...

PHILIP WOODERSON
Arf and the Happy Campers

Arf is now older and (a little) wiser and
ready to embark on his first hilarious
full-length adventure!

Arf expects to have to stay at home
during the school holidays while his
sisters enjoy a trip to France. However, the
plans go awry and he finds himself running
a camping ground and re-enacting
a battle between the Saxons
and the Normans!

Another fantastic Black Cat ...

FRANZESKA G. EWART
Bryony Bell
Tops the Bill

Bryony dreams of being a top-notch skater.
But she has to send back her new,
state-of-the-art skates to pay for her
sisters' costumes for *TV Family Star Turns*.
Poor Bryony. It's not much fun at school,
either. In the end of term play, she's cast
as the Ugly Ducking. Can the family's
fortunes – and Bryony's – turn in time
to give her the chance to strut her stuff?

Another fantastic Black Cat ...

CAROLINE PITCHER
THE GODS ARE WATCHING

Varro is a boy on the run. He's being
chased down the river Nile by a sinister
lord, and he doesn't know why.

Across water and over land,
and even in the deep tunnels beneath
the earth, he has no idea where
his journey will take him,or if
each footstep will bring him closer
to his death. This is an exciting, dramatic
mystery-adventure set in ancient Egypt,
by an award-winning writer.

Another fantastic Black Cat ...

REBECCA LISLE
Planimal Magic

Joe is staying with his cousins in the
country where his uncle runs a scientific
research institute. Late at night there's a
terrible, heart-stopping wail coming from
outside. Who – or what – is making it?

When Joe, his psychic dog, Bingo,
and cousin, Molly, embark on a search,
they make a magical, mysterious
discovery which some people will do
anything to keep secret ...

Another fantastic Black Cat ...

KAREN WALLACE
QUIRKY TIMES AT
QUAGMIRE CASTLE

Life couldn't be worse for Jack and
Emily. Quagmire Castle, their beloved,
crumbling home, is going to be sold.
Then they meet their long-lost ghostly
ancestors, and everything changes
overnight! Soon, it's all hands to the
pump to save Quagmire Castle –
with hilarious results no one could *ever*
have imagined!

Black Cats – collect them all!